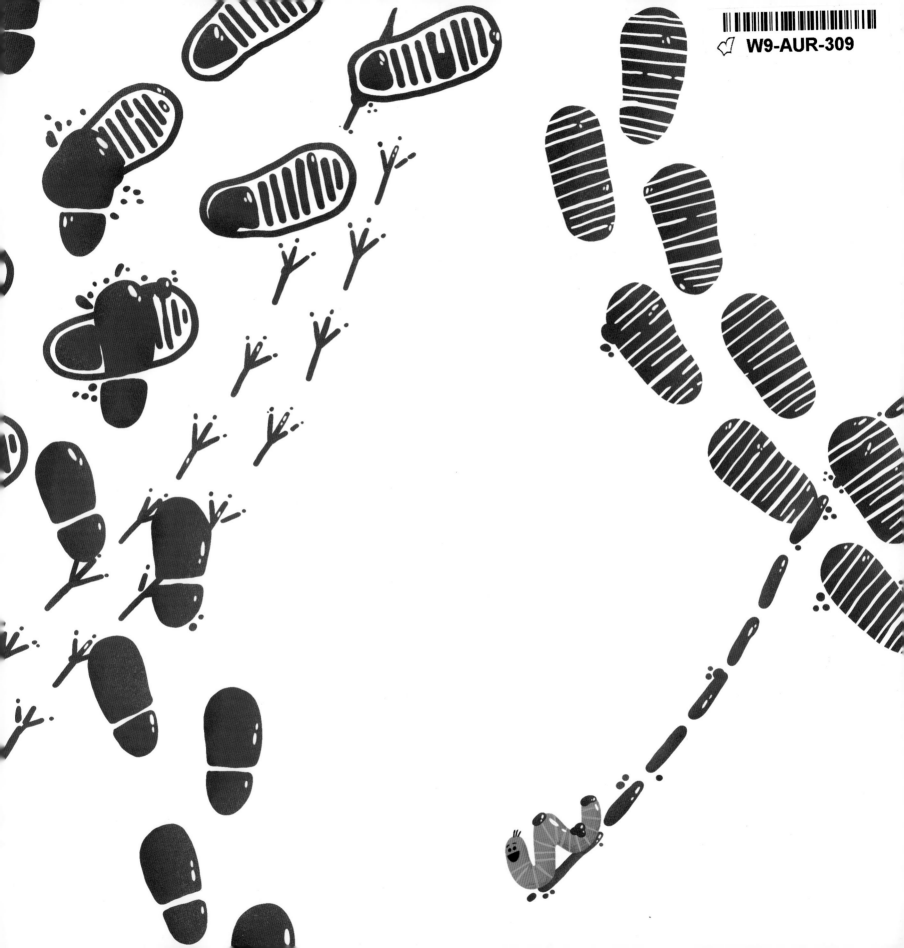

This book is dedicated to your mom.

Copyright © 2022 by Kristen Bell

Jacket art and interior illustrations by Daniel Wiseman

All rights reserved. Published in the United States by Random House Children's Books,
a division of Penguin Random House LLC, New York.

Random House and the colophon are registered trademarks of Penguin Random House LLC.

Visit us on the Web! rhcbooks.com

Educators and librarians, for a variety of teaching tools, visit us at RHTeachersLibrarians.com

ISBN 978-0-593-64295-5 (proprietary edition)

MANUFACTURED IN CHINA

10 9 8 7 6 5 4 3 2 1

The World Needs More PURPLE SCHOOLS

By **KRISTEN BELL & BENJAMIN HART**

Hey, kid. It's me, Penny Purple. Can I show you something stupendously ... fantastically ... pur-ple-eeee amazing?!

Illustrations by **DANIEL WISEMAN**

Random House 🏠 New York

Paaaa Pooow Blam! This is my school.

And guess what. . . .

My school is in the universe! That's right! THE UNIVERSE!

It's located right past the puppy-pirate galaxy, on planet Earth, next to some other floating space rocks and a big yellow sun.

But my school isn't just any plain ol' school in the universe.

My school is a **PURPLE SCHOOL**!

It's a place where lots of different people come together to mix their stories, their ideas, and their smarts to make something special.

(Yep! Just like when you mix red and blue together to make PURPLE!)

PURPLE DAY is in 2 Weeks!

I'm on a mission to help every school become a **PURPLE** school.

Is your school a **PURPLE** school? Do you want it to be?
Great! Let's get started.

To make your school **PURPLE**,

you have to start with wonder and curiosity.

Wonder & Curiosity

At my school, we like to wonder super-gigantic, universe-sized questions about the world.

No question is too big or too weird.

Could you make a burrito larger than a garbage truck?

TOY FOOD

Are there enough noses to smell all the smelly flowers in the entire world?

purple Garden

Do puppy pirates exist? And if so, do they like pizza?

Our questions are bigger than the biggest dinosaurs, the moon, and Frankie's dad.

But we also like to be curious and ask smaller, people-sized questions about our friends and our neighbors. So we can know their stories better!

Okay, it's time for Tell Us Your Story! Remember to be thinking up some good people-sized questions to ask Marvin when he's done!
ALL ABOUT ME

To make your school **PURPLE**, you also have to
roll up your sleeves and work really hard!

(And if you don't have sleeves, like Brian's mom,
that's okay, too.)

At my school, we know that we can learn anything
if we just get our brains working hard enough.

We don't always get it right the first time.

It takes even harder work to keep trying again and again.

But we also like to work hard to fix up our school and give back to the city that it's in.

Our school is an important part of our city, which is an important part of our country, which is an important part of our world, which is an important part of our universe!

Helping our school helps all of us!

LAVENDER
LAKE
PARK

Working hard is great, but did you know you ALSO need to be really silly to make your school **PURPLE**? You need to play. You need to laugh. And you HAVE to be what I like to call a captain wiggle-sillyton.

At my school, we like to play silly games.

And we like to use our imaginations.

We believe in a **PURPLE** world!

WALL DECAL

I am a
PURPLE
person!

WALL DECAL

You inspire me to be kind

when you

_____.

Thank you for sharing your
kindness with me when you

_____.

Thanks for being a **PURPLE**
person! You were very kind
when you

_____.

You make me feel special

when you

_____.

Mr. Tucker is always having dance parties to get our wiggles out, which ALSO gets our giggles out.

And Imani's new jokes make us shoot choco-milk out of our sniffers during lunch.

And then she said, "Just let it go. Let it goooo."

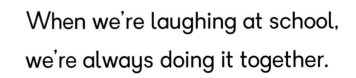

When we're laughing at school, we're always doing it together.

To make your school **PURPLE**, you have to be good at speaking up and using your voice!

But you also have to be good at listening to other people use their voices, too!

At my school, we don't always agree, and that's okay!

We always try to listen first, and then speak up for what we think is right.

No! I don't like the circus. I think we should have them dressed as historical characters.
We don't have to be against each other! We all want it to be really great. Can you tell us why you don't like the circus?
I don't think the animals are treated very nicely.
MEET OUR FURRY FRIENDS

Okay, are you ready for the final and most IMPORTANT way to make your school PURPLE?

JUST. BE. YOU!

The one and only you in the ENTIRE UNIVERSE.

That's right, when the one and only, curious and kind you adds your story . . . and your ideas . . . and your smarts to your school . . . it helps us all learn more things about the world we live in and the people we live here with. And that helps our world get bigger and our world get better!

And that's why I think the world needs more **PURPLE** schools.